http://www.randomhouse.com/

Library of Congress Cataloging-in-Publication Data
Sadler, Marilyn.
Honey Bunny Funnybunny / by Marilyn Sadler ; illustrated by Roger Bollen.
   p.   cm. "Beginner Books."
SUMMARY: Honey Bunny Funnybunny feels that something is missing when her bothersome big brother finally stops teasing her.
ISBN: 0-679-88181-6 (trade) — ISBN 0-679-98181-0 (lib. bdg.)
[1. Brothers and sisters—Fiction.   2. Rabbits—Fiction.]
I. Bollen, Roger, ill.   II. Title.
PZ7.S1239Ho   1997
[E]—dc20
96-16735

                                                                    24

Honey Bunny Funnybunny

by Marilyn Sadler

illustrated by Roger Bollen

BEGINNER BOOKS
A Division of Random House, Inc.

Honey Bunny Funnybunny
had a big brother.
His name was P. J. Funnybunny.

P. J. Funnybunny loved
Honey Bunny Funnybunny
very much.
But he liked to tease her.

Every morning,
P. J. pulled the covers
off Honey Bunny's bed.

Sometimes he poured orange juice
on her cornflakes.

He liked to tie knots
in the sleeves of her pretty dresses.

He poured blue paint
in her yellow paint jar.

And yellow paint
in her blue paint jar.

He even switched the heads
on her dolls.

And every night at the dinner table,
P. J. smashed mashed carrots
on poor Honey Bunny's head!

After dinner, he put
her favorite fuzzy bunny blanket
in the freezer.

At bedtime, he hid under her bed
and yelled, "Boo!"

"At least P. J. can't bother me
while I'm sleeping!"
said Honey Bunny Funnybunny.

Then one night...

...while Honey Bunny
was fast asleep...

...P. J. painted her face bright green.

"Mom!" cried Honey Bunny
in the morning.
"Look what P. J. did!"

Mr. Funnybunny was very angry.
He sent P. J. to his room.

"You are a very bad bunny!"
Mrs. Funnybunny said.

After that, things were different
at the Funnybunny house.

Honey Bunny had her cornflakes
with milk.

Her pretty dresses
stayed nice and pretty.

With her blue and yellow paints,
she painted big yellow suns
in blue skies.

Honey Bunny's dolls
kept their own heads.

P. J. Funnybunny had stopped teasing
Honey Bunny Funnybunny.

At first Honey Bunny
was very happy.

But after a while,
she began to feel
that something was missing.

"Where is P. J.?"
she asked her mother one day.
"He's gone out to play
with his friends,"
said Mrs. Funnybunny.

Honey Bunny sat down by the window.

She did not want to paint.

She did not want to play dolls.

She did not even want to play
with her friends.

She sat and sat and waited
for P. J. to come home.

Finally, P. J. came up the walk.

"Hi, P. J.!" said Honey Bunny.

But P. J. went right past
Honey Bunny.

That night at dinner, P. J. sat
and ate his mashed carrots.
Honey Bunny just stared at hers.

When it was time for bed,
Honey Bunny's fuzzy bunny blanket
was soft and warm.
But Honey Bunny did not care.

Honey Bunny looked
under her bed.
No P. J.
No "Boo!"

The next morning,
P. J. did not pull the covers
off Honey Bunny's bed.
Honey Bunny was as sad
as sad can be.

"Mom!" she cried.

"P.J. doesn't love me anymore!"

Mrs. Funnybunny looked
at Honey Bunny.
Then she smiled.
"Oh, yes, he does," she said.
"Come with me."

Mrs. Funnybunny
took Honey Bunny
into the bathroom.

She lifted her up
in front of the mirror.

Honey Bunny could not believe
her eyes!
Her face was painted blue
with yellow polka dots!

"P. J. loves me!" she cried.
Honey Bunny Funnybunny
was very happy.

She ran to P. J.'s room.
"P. J. Funnybunny,
you are the best brother
a bunny could ever have!"
said Honey Bunny Funnybunny.

And she gave him
a great big fuzzy bunny hug.

Try all of these great
Beginner Book stories:

ANTHONY THE PERFECT MONSTER
by Angelo DeCesare

ARE YOU MY MOTHER?
by P. D. Eastman

THE BEAR DETECTIVES
by Stan and Jan Berenstain

THE CAT IN THE HAT
by Dr. Seuss

GREEN EGGS AND HAM
by Dr. Seuss

IT'S NOT EASY BEING A BUNNY
by Marilyn Sadler

I WISH THAT I HAD DUCK FEET
by Theo. LeSieg

NEW TRICKS I CAN DO!
by Robert Lopshire

STOP, TRAIN, STOP!
A Thomas the Tank Engine Story
Based on *The Railway Series*
by the Rev. W. Awdry

THE VERY BAD BUNNY
by Marilyn Sadler